a magical bedtime story

WRITTEN BY Erin Rovin

ILLUSTRATED by Katie Campbell

RIVER ROAD PRESS

New Orleans 2018

First edition, 2017
First River Road Press edition, 2018

ISBN: 978-1-941879-17-7

The name and logo for "River Road Press" are trademarks of River Road Press LLC and are registered with the U.S. Patent and Trademark Office.

For information regarding permission to reproduce selections from this book, write to Permissions, River Road Press LLC, PO Box 125, Metairie, Louisiana 70004.

For information on other River Road Press titles, please visit www.riverroadpress.com.

Printed in Korea

Published by River Road Press
PO Box 125
Metairie, LA 70004

"This book is a charming way to teach children about ordinary and practical magic, the wisdom of elders, and friendships with animals."

—*Martha C. Ward*

DEDICATED TO
Marie, for inspiration.
Russell, for making it possible.
Sam, for making it a reality.
And Story, for making it worthwhile.

My name is Little Laveau. I was born on the banks of the Mississippi River. I have many pets and lots of friends. I help all my friends when they have troubles. And I just seem to find pets!

But I sometimes get into trouble. I know it when I hear my Grams holler,

"Little Laveau!"

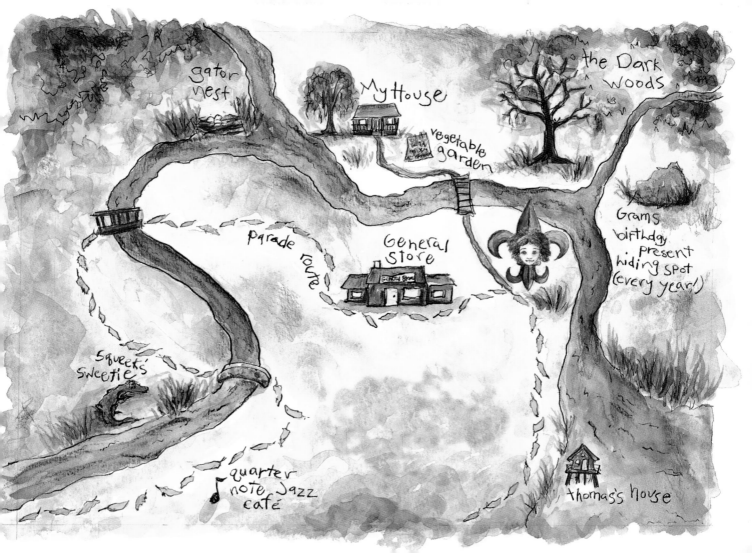

I hadn't seen my best friend Thomas
for a few days so me and Squeeker—
that's my pet alligator—we decided
to go and pay Thomas a visit . . .

Do you wanna hear
how I got Squeeker?

I always wanted a pet gator and my Grams said, "If you come across a gator with no teeth *then* you can keep him."

And wouldn't you know it, I did just that!

I found a whole bunch of baby gators last spring. They all followed their mama into the muddy water except for one scrawny, crazy little guy who made squeaky noises.

When he opened his mouth there wasn't one pointy gator tooth! I kept an eye out and fed him every day for three whole months until he got bigger and bigger and then he followed me home. He still had no teeth so I knew Grams couldn't say no.

When Grams saw Squeeker walking up to our house, she came out screamin', *"Little Laveau!* Run inside! There's a gator behind you!"

"Thaa-at's right," I laughed. Grams kept a close eye on us but she let me keep him. A promise is a promise.

And that's how I got Squeeker! Okay, so now back to Thomas . . .

Thomas was sitting on his porch painting a picture of . . . well, it didn't really look like much but a swirl of colors. Squeeker started to sun himself in front of some marshmallows that quickly turned into goo from the heat.

Thomas looked so sad. It just wasn't like him. He was usually joking and chasing the other kids with worms and bullfrogs. So I sat down.

"Thomas, are you okay?" I said as I inspected his mix of colors that had turned a Squeek shade of green.

"I'm having bad dreams," Thomas said. "I don't want to go to sleep because I'm afraid I will have a nightmare."

"Well," I said. "I know a thing or two about nightmares!"

"You see, I used to get them so bad my Grams would whip up a special tea from a special root that helped until I figured out there's no need to be afraid! All bad dreams are swept away to make something beautiful."

"When you have a bad dream, gather up all those bad thoughts and put them in a jar. Take that jar and sprinkle those dreams right down the drain. They flow through the rivers and out into the sea. The salt water washes them clean and takes out all the scary."

"Then they get swept up onto the beach as grains of sand, where the sun warms the bad right out of them all day long. That's what the beautiful beach is made of! Bad dreams turned good and wonderful by the ocean and the sun."

I ran fast across the lawn and over the bridge dividing our houses. I flew through the front door with Grams yelling, *"Close the screen door!"*

I went into my room and fished out one of my jam jars that Grams gave me. Then I ran back to Thomas's house.

He was so excited to get his new dream jar so he could fill it up and dump his bad dreams down the drain.

The next morning my pet rooster—Rooster—woke me with his rooster call. I threw him some rice and cleaned up fast because I was so eager to see how Thomas's night was!

As soon as I had finished breakfast, Grams' special cinnamon buns, I took off with Squeeker across the bridge to Thomas's house.

Thomas greeted me with a huge hug and said, "Oh Little Laveau! How did you know? It worked like a charm! No bad dreams for me last night!"

"And I wasn't afraid to sleep because I knew what to do with the dreams if they were bad!"

Grams' *Good Dream* Tea Recipe

—It's mostly just Chamomile.

—Add some Rose Petals (to dream of all things lovely).

—Then add 1 tsp. of raw Lavender Honey (to dream of all things sweet)

Dream Jar Journal

Date of dream:

Tell me all about it . . .

_____

_____

_____

_____

_____

_____

_____

_____

_____

Dream Jar Journal

Date of dream:

Tell me all about it . . .

_____

_____

_____

_____

_____

_____

_____

_____

_____

Dream Jar Journal

Date of dream:

Tell me all about it . . .

_____

_____

_____

_____

_____

_____

_____

_____

Dream  Journal

Date of dream:

Tell me all about it . . .

_____

_____

_____

_____

_____

_____

_____

_____

Dream Jar Journal

Date of dream:

Tell me all about it . . .

_____
_____
_____
_____
_____
_____
_____
_____
_____

Join Little Laveau and her new bayou friends in

Bayou Beware!

Available now!